# HAPPY MAGIC FOREST

## AND THE DEEP TROUBLE

For the seas; let's make it our
quest to look after them.

# OXFORD
**UNIVERSITY PRESS**

Great Clarendon Street, Oxford OX2 6DP

Oxford University Press is a department of the University of Oxford.
It furthers the University's objective of excellence in research, scholarship,
and education by publishing worldwide. Oxford is a registered trade mark of
Oxford University Press in the UK and in certain other countries

British Library Cataloguing in Publication Data

Data available

ISBN: 978-0-19-277750-8

1 3 5 7 9 10 8 6 4 2

Printed in China

Paper used in the production of this book is a natural,
recyclable product made from wood grown in sustainable forests.

The manufacturing process conforms to the environmental
regulations of the country of origin.

# SUPER HAPPY MAGIC FOREST

### MATTY LONG

## AND THE DEEP TROUBLE

OXFORD
UNIVERSITY PRESS

# THE SUPER HAPPY HEROES

## Hoofius (faun)

A delightful mix of pointy and furry bits, Hoofius likes to take on the role of leader of the heroes. He takes questing very seriously and holds nothing but contempt for clothes and personal grooming.

## Blossom (unicorn)

A champion frolicker, Blossom is impulsive and likes to live in the moment. His unpredictable nature surprises friends and enemies alike.

He also eats like a horse.

## Twinkle (fairy)

The only airborne member of the group, Twinkle is a useful scout and surprisingly strong for her size. She's also easily distracted by anything cute or shiny.

## Herbert (gnome)

Rake-wielder and packer of picnics. Questing without Herbert would likely see you lost, hungry, and unable to identify wild flowers.

## Trevor (mushroom)

Small, squishy, and great in an omelette; what Trevor lacks in size and limbs, he makes up for in smart ideas and sharp one-liners.

# CHAPTER ONE
# SOMETHING FISHY

This story begins in the SUPER HAPPY MAGIC FOREST. You may have heard of it. After all, it was number one on the latest 'Top Ten Places to Frolic' list and was awarded five golden stars in the *Best Places to be a Gnome* guide. You can't argue with that. I mean, you *really* can't. Nobody argues in the SUPER HAPPY MAGIC FOREST. They're too busy picnicking in the woods or singing from the hilltops or dancing in the meadows.

And sometimes, they're underwater . . .

Indeed, it was the morning of the Super-Dive-a-Thon, when residents celebrated their forest's pristine waters by searching the depths of Lake Sparkle for the tasty treasures that grew there. Each resident was allowed to pluck just one treasure for themselves. The event martial, Tiddlywink the pixie, would see to that.

No cannonballing! Once you take a treasure, please leave the lake. I SAID NO CANNONBALLING!

Being a magic forest lake, you'd be sure to find more than just pebbles and old boots below the surface. Delicious candy coral and glitterweed grew there, as well as rare lollipops and giant sherbet shells. It all made for a great day out, as long as you kept your wits about you.

Hoofius was determined to find something extra special this year. Especially after last time . . .

His eyes darted as he combed the lake floor while ignoring the usual sweet temptations. Before long, he had swum far away from the Tiddlywink-approved diving zone. And then he saw it.

The mysterious creature drifted in the water, clutching a tiny trident and not looking very alive. Hoofius gathered the creature under his arm.

'I've found something!' he spluttered as he splashed and kicked his way past his friends to the bank of the lake. They followed, excited to see what it was. It surely had to be an improvement on last year's effort.

Other folk began to gather around, and the murmuring and gasping began.

'COULD A MEDICAL ATTENDANT PLEASE MAKE THEMSELVES KNOWN?' blasted Tiddlywink on his megaphone.

The crowd parted as a mushroom stepped through. Sporting a stethoscope and a pair of tight-fitting trunks, it was clear Dr Shroomsworth had come prepared for both work *and* play.

He knelt beside the creature, examining it from top to tail.

It's okay, everyone. The doctor is in.

11

'Hmmm . . .' mused the mushroom. 'Humanoid top half . . . head, eyes . . . arms. But as for those gills and the tail . . . let's just say there's something fishy going on here.'

'FOR GOODNESS' SAKE, SHROOMSWORTH! IS IT *ALIVE?*' boomed Tiddlywink, enjoying his new toy. The crowd winced as the racket rattled through their ears. The creature startled awake from the noise.

'Nope. Definitely dead,' replied the doctor, turning back to his patient.

Water . . .
please . . .

'WAH!' cried Shroomsworth, stumbling backwards in alarm.

Hoofius carefully lifted the creature and plopped it down into a barrel of water. It dove down to the bottom and then resurfaced, enjoying the feeling of water over its skin. And then it spoke.

'Phew, that's better. Merfolk aren't great with the whole "being on dry land" thing. It makes us go a bit crispy.'

'I knew it!' said Herbert excitedly. 'I've read about the merfolk before. But you live out in the deep sea. What brings you here?'

'AND MORE IMPORTANTLY, WHY DIDN'T YOU SIGN IN ON THE VISITOR'S LOGBOOK?' added Tiddlywink, unimpressed.

But Fishopolis is no longer safe for merfolk. The Singing Pearl can no longer be heard because the big clam it sits in was shut tight by a SEA WITCH!

And now evil things have moved in and sent the merfolk into hiding, afraid that they will be captured... or worse.

'I swam the seas looking for help,' continued Foam. And when I couldn't find any, I journeyed all the way upstream to this forest lake. And that's when you found me, tired and exhausted.'

'Well, you have come to the right place!' chimed in Blossom. 'My friends and I have done plenty of quests. We can help!'

'Ahem!' interrupted Tiddlywink, lowering the megaphone. 'I don't mean to sit on your cupcakes or anything, but this *fish-whopper-lis* place is deep underwater.
And correct me if I'm wrong, but none of you can breathe underwater!'

Foam giggled. Or gurgled. (It was hard to tell.) She looked at the heroes.

'Have you ever heard of . . . *mersonification?*'

CHAPTER TWO

# ENTER THE CENTAUR

As it happened, the heroes had never
heard of mersonification, and Foam
quickly found out that the Super Happy Magic
Forest folk treated big long words with much
suspicion.

'Everything will be made clear once you
meet the Mer-mage of Merhaven,' she
assured them. 'But I must rest here.' And so
it was that a short while later, the heroes
found themselves sitting on a boat, heading
downriver on a new quest to the open sea.

After a slight (delicious) detour, the heroes steered the boat back on course. And it was not just any boat. This was the SS Tiddly: the personal pleasure barge of Tiddlywink the pixie and hand-carved by

18

the best gnome carpenters. One might suspect that Tiddlywink had secret motives for lending the heroes his own boat. Such a show of generosity in public certainly boosted his approval ratings as a councillor, and he'd be the first to tell everyone that he played a major part in a successful quest. After all, it was the finest vessel in the land.

Water sloshed at their feet as they steered
the boat on to a sandbank, where Herbert
gave it a once-over with his magnifying glass.

'Ah! There's the hole.
We need something
soft and foamy
to plug the gap.'

Why are you
all looking at
me?

As the heroes thought harder
about how to fix the hole,
there was a rustle in the bushes
nearby, and out stepped a group
of bandits.

Hehe! Hand
over your
stuff!

The heroes backed away until there was nowhere to run.

'Hoofius, what do we do?' whispered Twinkle. Hoofius stared at the unfriendly-looking things that were pointing at them. He tried to speak but could only come out with wobbly-lipped nonsense. He didn't know what to do. And he was scared.

# 'AAAEEE–OOO–AH–AH–EEEEEEEEE!'

A battle cry sounded. A mighty warrior was charging right at the bandits, swinging a huge sword.

The heroes watched, stunned, as a battle began.

Soon the bandits had dropped their weapons and were running scared. The warrior boomed with laughter as they fled.

'WOW! That was . . . incredible!' stammered Hoofius.

The stranger snorted. 'They were just hobgoblin bandits. Try battling ten ogre warriors at once. Never levelled up so fast in my life. Anyway, who are you? Fans of mine, I presume. Look, Horsius the Mighty doesn't do autographs, but you can have this.'

He took out a towel and wiped the sweat from his face and armpits before flinging it at Hoofius.

. . . Thank you.

23

'Does anyone else want a towel?' he asked.

The other heroes shook their heads. Hoofius peeled the towel off his face and stared at the warrior with wide-eyed amazement.

Half man, half horse? Well now I've seen everything!

We're called centaurs. But I'm more of a cen-PHWOAR!

'Thank you for dealing with those bandits,' said Hoofius eagerly. 'We are in your debt!'

'I didn't do it for you,' said the centaur. 'I did it for glory! And the thrill of battle! Anyway, if you aren't Horsius the Mighty fans, then who are you?'

'We're heroes on an epic quest,' said Hoofius.

The centaur boomed with laughter. Hoofius suddenly felt a bit foolish.

'Oh, you were serious?' said Horsius the Mighty. 'Well then, why don't you join me at my campfire, and you can tell me all about this quest of yours over some toasted marshmallows.'

The heroes followed him to his camp and settled themselves down as Horsius the Mighty bragged for what seemed like an eternity. The heroes couldn't get a word in edgeways.

You're staring at a five-times Adventurer of the Year winner. I once defeated a fire genie, saved a penguin village from an avalanche, and completed twelve side quests all before breakfast.

Finally, it was the heroes' turn.

'Anyway, Hoopus, have you lot battled any worthy foes, or am I the only mighty warrior around here?'

'Err . . . of course,' said Hoofius, ignoring the mispronunciation of his name. 'There was the time we defeated an evil slug, and there was a mega mushroom that—'

'Slugs? Mushrooms? HA HA HA! Good one, Hoopus. Not bad for a *BEGINNER*!'

'We're going to defeat a sea witch!' Hoofius blurted in response, eager to impress.

'Hmmm, sounds like a worthy foe,' said the centaur. 'And I bet there'll be some kind of reward at the end of it! How about I join you? I get the glory and treasure, and you amateurs can get a load of what it's like to battle beside a five-times Adventurer of the Year winner!'

Hoofius's ears pricked up at the sound of that. Well, further than usual. He hadn't forgotten the fear he'd felt when up against the bandits. Maybe it was time for him to toughen up and learn a new approach. Maybe *Hoofius* could be Adventurer of the Year one day!

'Sure, it would be an honour,' said Hoofius, as the centaur nodded approvingly. But the other heroes weren't so sure.

Psst. At least he has marshmallows!

# CHAPTER THREE
# JIGGING FOR TREASURE

The next morning found the heroes back in the SS Tiddly, heading downriver towards the sea. All apart from Twinkle, who had to fly to make way for the formidable frame of Horsius the Mighty.

Thanks, Tinkle!

It's TWINKLE!

A marshmallow plugged the leaky hole,
and so far it was keeping them afloat as
Hoofius outlined the quest to Horsius
the Mighty.

'We must travel to Fishopolis to defeat the
Sea Witch. But first, we need to get to
Merhaven and find the Mer-mage. Without
his help, we won't be able to breathe
underwater.'

The river spat them out into a big
empty ocean.

'This doesn't look right,' said Herbert,
squinting into the distance. 'Foam said
Merhaven would be visible from the
shore. The river did split in two at one
point. Maybe we went the wrong way!'

The group frantically paddled to a town on the shore and found it inhabited by strange-looking folk. They certainly didn't look like the frolicking kind.

Ooh! I want an earring!

Pirates! The bandits of the seas.

'They'll steal the boat if we're not careful! Pirates are always doing things like that,' said Horsius the Mighty. 'I'll have to fight them.'

The heroes already had a leaking boat and a lack of directions to Merhaven to worry about without the centaur charging in and swinging his sword around.

'Maybe you could stay here and guard the boat?' asked Herbert, keen to keep Horsius the Mighty out of trouble.

'I'll help!' said Hoofius, his fists clenched.

'That's the spirit, Hoopus!' The centaur slapped him on the back. It felt like being hit by a cannonball.

Herbert rummaged in his pack and pulled out a leak-fixing kit.

He gave it to Hoofius. 'Just in case you get a break from fighting off pirates,' Herbert said, with a wink. Then he and the three remaining heroes wandered into town to look for a guidebook.

The sound of music and merriment drifted out of a tavern nearby.

'Do you hear that?' squealed Blossom.

'It sounds like . . . FROLICKING!'

Blossom barged inside, unable to contain his
excitement. There were pirates everywhere,
drinking from huge barrels and cheering
as two of the pirates danced around on
a table as though their lives depended on
it. Suddenly, the music stopped playing and
everyone fell silent. Only a colourful bird in
the corner spoke.

BwAAAArk!
JIGGIN' JOE IS THE
WINNER! HAND OVER
YOUR GOLD!

The crowd cheered, and the losing pirate
handed over a pouch of gold coins to the
winner.

'It looks like a . . . frolicking competition?'
said Twinkle, as the winning pirate
celebrated. He threw his head back and
hollered a new challenge.

Who here be
next to challenge
Jiggin' Joe?

ME!

'The rules be simple!' said Jiggin' Joe. 'When
the music plays, we be jiggin'. When the
music stops, no more jiggin' ye be doin'!
Whoever impresses Captain Beaky the

most wins. The loser hands over his booty. Savvy?'

Blossom smiled and nodded. He didn't understand a word.

'If ye beat me, I'll give ye my magic compass that points to wherever ye tell it to. And if ye lose, how abouts ye give me that shiny golden horn o' yours?'

A chorus of 'oooooh' and 'arrrrrr!' went up from the crowd as they stared at Blossom's horn. Jiggin' Joe chuckled and revealed his toothless mouth.

Wouldn't you rather have my teeth? You look like you need some.

The pirate's face screwed up in rage. 'WHAT!? Nobody be talkin' to Jiggin' Joe like that! How abouts I just take the horn right now?'

He drew his cutlass just as the music started up, but Blossom was already on the move.

Get back here, ye fancy pony!

Blossom leapt from table to table, twisting and twirling as if he'd never left the frolicking fields of home. Jiggin' Joe scrambled after him, poking his cutlass at empty air and shouting angry-sounding words that would make an ogre blush.

The other heroes watched in awe at the performance, but Blossom wasn't done yet. He steadied himself, crouched down, and launched into his big finish.

His friends knew it well.

## THE MEGA RAINBOW HORN-SPIN.

The move had been banned in the Super Happy Magic Forest ever since a nasty accident resulted in three gnomes and a pixie being airlifted to Dr Shroomsworth's surgery. Blossom was still spinning as the music cut, and everyone turned to Captain Beaky.

BWAAAARK!
FANCY PONY IS
THE WINNER!

Blossom was swept up on the shoulders of cheering pirates, and someone wrenched the prized compass from Jiggin' Joe's neck and placed it around the unicorn. Then a brawl broke out, and the heroes found themselves crawling under a mass of flying hooks and peg legs towards the way out.

Hoofius had just fixed the SS Tiddly when his friends burst into view, with a furious-looking Jiggin' Joe following in the distance.

'Are we leaving already?' asked the faun, as his friends clattered into the boat.

'Put it this way,' said Trevor, catching his breath. 'I don't think we'll be staying for an encore.'

## CHAPTER FOUR
# IN A PINCH

'You *ran* from a pirate brawl?' asked Horsius the Mighty, as Trevor recounted the events from the town. 'That sounds cowardly to me. I would have given 'em a few more hooks for hands!' He sliced the air with his sword.

The group had put some distance between themselves and the toothless rage of Jiggin' Joe, and the SS Tiddly was going strong over the waves thanks to Hoofius's handiwork with the repair kit.

Herbert held the enchanted compass.

He whispered 'Merhaven' and watched in amazement as the dial spun and settled on a direction.

'Works like a charm!' chirped the gnome.

Unfortunately for the heroes, it didn't account for any obstacles they might encounter along the way.

They were headed straight for a whirlpool.

They crashed in a heap on an island nearby and watched as the SS Tiddly disappeared on its final voyage to the bottom of the sea.

'Well, it had a good run,' said Trevor.

'We're going to be in so much trouble,' said Hoofius. He could only imagine the shades of red Tiddlywink's face would go through when he learnt about this.

'Should have let me fight it,' said Horsius the Mighty. 'I once wrestled a mountain. A whirlpool would have been no match for me!'

'Then maybe you should have stayed in the boat!' snapped Twinkle. Her arms felt like

they could drop off, and she was in no mood
for the centaur right now.

Hoofius seemed happy to have a legendary
warrior with them, but the other heroes
weren't so sure. They had never travelled
with someone who, left alone, could
probably find a reason to fight his own tail.

What did
you call
me?

The heroes of the Super Happy Magic Forest certainly didn't go *looking* for battles like Horsius the Mighty did. He was a different kind of hero entirely.

Clack! Clack! Clack!

'Can anyone else hear that?' asked Trevor.

The sound of skittering and scraping and clack-clack-clacking was coming from beyond a row of palm trees.

They weren't alone on the island.

Look!

'They've captured a merperson!' said
Hoofius. Their captive was a sorry sight,
weakly trying to drag itself away before
finding its tail trapped under the weight
of a large pincer.

'If it doesn't get back into the water, it'll dry out,' whispered Twinkle.

'Not if they eat it first,' added Blossom unhelpfully.

51

'We need a plan,' said Hoofius urgently.

'Too late,' observed Trevor. 'The Horsius has bolted.'

The centaur galloped into the crabs at full speed, and claws and pincers flew off in all directions.

As the crabs scattered, the centaur
reached down and picked up the merperson.

'He's saved it! Bravo!' clapped Herbert, and
the heroes breathed a sigh of relief. But
then Horsius the Mighty began swinging
the merperson around by the tail, before
unleashing it high and far towards
the sea.

'That's one way of stopping it from drying
out,' said Trevor, as they watched the
merperson fly through the air and land in
the ocean.

The warrior clapped his hands together at a job well done. 'IS THERE NO ONE STRONG ENOUGH TO BATTLE HORSIUS THE MIGHTY?' he roared.

The ground beneath him began to shake. Below the sand, something was rising to the challenge.

Errr...it was really more of a rhetorical question...

# LAYING DOWN
# THE CLAW

'So . . . you must be Clawdius!' said Horsius the Mighty, remembering the crabs' conversation from moments before.

'And *you* must be frightened!' the colossal crab replied. Foam dripped from his mouth, and he clacked his claws together. The sound gave the heroes the shivers. You wouldn't want to find yourself caught up in those.

'Come closer, little horse-man! I'll give you a much-needed haircut!' spat the crab.

The centaur dodged and swerved as pincers snapped inches away from his head. Every swing of his sword simply glanced off the hardened shell of Clawdius.

Horsius the Mighty backed away until he found himself pinned against a palm tree. He gave it a quick kick with his hind legs, and a coconut fell into his waiting hand.

He drew back his arm and hurled it.

Ha ha! A coconut KO!

57

Clawdius lay twitching in the sand, knocked out cold. The heroes cautiously approached Horsius the Mighty.

'That was amazing!' said Hoofius. 'Can you teach me to do that?'

'Probably not,' said the centaur. 'When it comes to battle, you either have it, or you don't. And I've seen buttercups with more fight in them than you five.'

Hoofius looked crushed. 'We were about to join in!' he blurted. 'We've got through plenty of battles!'

He was interrupted by loud slurping sounds, and for a moment they wondered if Clawdius was back on his feet.

'You've got through plenty of desserts, more like!' roared the centaur.

'Hey! Quests aren't all about battling, you know,' said Twinkle.

'Indeed. They're also about the loot!' came the response, and Horsius the Mighty began searching the crab's camp for anything shiny or expensive-looking to take away.

'Hoofius!' whispered Twinkle once the centaur was out of earshot. 'Are you sure that Horsius the Mighty is so great? He's rude and a big show-off!'

'I have to agree,' said Herbert, joining them. 'And he has no appreciation for the art of gardening. It took me half an hour to explain to him what a rake was for.'

'You do go on a bit, though,' added Trevor.

'If you ask me . . .' said Blossom, in between licking coconut juice off his hooves, 'I don't think Horsius the Mighty really cares about helping others at all.'

Blossom thumped a nearby palm tree and held his hoof out expectantly.

'He just has a different questing style,' replied Hoofius defensively, as Trevor shot Blossom an unimpressed look.

'Imagine what we could learn from a five-times Adventurer of the Year!' he continued. 'Maybe we've been doing it wrong this whole time. Maybe we need to be tougher and braver and ready to battle for glory!' He swung his fists around as if mimicking a master battler delivering a finishing blow to their enemy.

'That's a start!' observed Horsius the Mighty, rejoining the group. 'Though you might want to throw in a kick or two. And if you really want to catch them off guard . . .'

He leaned in and whispered something secret in Hoofius's ear. Whatever it was, the faun looked excited that such a great warrior would pass on such sacred knowledge.

'I hope you're whispering ideas on how to get off this island,' said Trevor.

Hoofius's stomach sank when he remembered the fate of the SS Tiddly. Among the crab-bashing and coconut-throwing, everyone had forgotten about *that* particular problem.

As they walked back towards the shore, they noticed something waving at them from the water.
It was the merperson that had been flying through the sky moments earlier.

'My name is Kelp,' she said after the heroes had introduced themselves.
'I must thank you for my rescue. It was quite the
. . . thrill ride.'

Glad I could KELP! Ha ha!

Kelp was excited to hear that the heroes had met Foam and were on a quest to Merhaven. She filled them in on her own perilous journey in which she nearly ended up as crab food.

'I escaped from Fishopolis after the Pearl Song stopped but was sniffed out and chased by hungry shark guards into unfamiliar seas. That's when the crabs caught me.'

At the mention of sharks, five fins appeared in the water behind Kelp and advanced rapidly towards her.

'LOOK OUT!' cried Hoofius.

Kelp was tossed into the air, again and again.

But she appeared to be enjoying herself.

'Kelp, we-ee-ee really must get going!' said the lead dolphin, as the fun died down. 'These waters aren't safe!'

Kelp turned to the heroes. 'I hope you don't mind getting a bit wet . . .'

65

The thrill of dolphin riding was like nothing the heroes had ever experienced. And they had been down rainbow slides and eaten from ice cream trees. It was only Herbert who didn't seem to be enjoying himself.

Stop the ride! I want to get off!

But the dolphins weren't about to slow down.

They were being followed.

## CHAPTER SIX
# MERHAVEN

There were five in total. All jagged teeth, sharp fins, and pointy bits. They clutched weapons too and could swim much faster than dolphins being weighed down by various other creatures.

Shark guards.

'Those swords don't really seem necessary,' observed Trevor, as the shark guards closed to within chomping distance.

'We're nearly-ee-ee there!' squealed the lead dolphin. A rocky outcrop began to loom in front of them. 'Hold on!'

The next thing they knew, they were in the air.

WAHOOO!

They cleared the rocky barrier that surrounded the refuge of Merhaven, and the next moments passed in a blur of falling through air and flailing in water.

The dolphins nudged and prodded the heroes on to firm ground, who had taken on a lot of extra water.

When they had finally composed themselves, their eyes could take in their surroundings for the first time.

Dozens of little mer-heads blinked back at them from the water.

'What are they staring at?' wondered Horsius the Mighty, rinsing seawater from his hair. 'Have you fish-people never seen a horse-man flying through the air on a dolphin before?'

As it happened, they hadn't. But they were delighted to see Kelp back safely, and she introduced the group as the heroes who were going to save Fishopolis. A lot of gasping and gurgling sounds followed as the merfolk reacted to the news.

And then one by one, they began to introduce themselves.

I get it! You're all named after what's on your head!

Nope. I'm Dave.

'A merperson takes an oath to always protect and look after the part of the sea they choose to wear on their head,' came an older-sounding voice. 'Within reason, of course. We had a merperson called Shark once. It didn't end well.'

I'm Barnacle. But some call me the Mer-mage.

The other merfolk moved aside to let the older one through.

76

He looked them up and down and then spoke.

'So, we sent Foam to ask for help, and you answered her call, hmm? You're not quite what we were expecting. You haven't even got any fishy parts! But then, I suppose we can help with that.' He chuckled.

'Enough riddles, Grandpa!' blurted Horsius the Mighty. 'Can we just skip to the part where I defeat the Sea Witch, and you give me a nice reward? I tire of all the fleeing and hiding and . . . FISH!' He picked out a small fry that had got tangled up in his hair and tossed it into the water.

The Mer-mage frowned.

Hoofius spoke up. 'What Horsius the Mighty means to say is, we are keen to try and help the merfolk in any way we can!'

'In *any way* you can . . .' mused the Mermage. 'Yes, indeed, you will! Then let us not waste any more time. The mer-queendom hereby accepts your offer of help.' He turned to face the merfolk and raised his arms.

LET THE MERSONIFICATION CEREMONY BEGIN!

Around them the merfolk began to gurgle,
creating bubbles with their mouths that
floated up into the air.
It was an unnerving
sight, but not everyone
was troubled by it.

Woohoo!
Bubbles!

- pop! -

The gurgling soon
swelled to a cacophony.
The heroes could only just
make out the voice of
the Mer-mage above it.

'The time has come for you to become
one with the salt and surf! Shepherds
of the shallows and deeps! To become
honorary members of the mer-queendom!
Drink from this vial, and discover your . . .
*mersona*!'

'Let me have a go!' said Blossom, grabbing the vial from the Mer-mage and taking a huge gulp.

'Well?' asked Twinkle.

BUUURP!

'Tastes like Tiddlywink's feet,' said Blossom, his face curling.

'But do you *feel* any different?' asked Herbert.

'I don't think . . .' said Blossom, his voice trailing off. His skin started to feel dry. Breathing became harder. He collapsed to his knees.

'Something's happening!' he gasped.

## CHAPTER SEVEN
# A TWIST IN THE TAIL

In the moments that followed, Blossom found himself overcome with a need to dive. The water was calling to him.

So in he jumped.

Blossom slammed back into the water and soon burst out again, this time performing a front flip in the air. The dolphins and merfolk applauded the sight.

'Excellent!' cried the Mer-mage. 'Now the rest of you. The watery world awaits!'

The other heroes each took a sip from the vial and were overcome with the same sensations. It created *quite* the tidal wave.

AHHHH!

Soon they reappeared, though not all had quite the same level of gusto as Blossom.

'Behold your **mersonas!**' cried the Mer-mage triumphantly.

Where did you all go? What trickery is this?

How does this work?

The group had been granted various flippers, fins, tails, and tentacles to help them swim, and gills to let them breathe underwater. They took quite a bit of getting used to.

Luckily, the dolphins were there to provide expert coaching.

Once the excitement and bubble-blowing had died down, the Mer-mage spoke up. There was great sadness in his voice.

'You heroes have heard of the Sea Witch that has taken over Fishopolis. The truth is, there is more to this than we'd like to admit . . .'

He bowed his head, and a hush fell over Merhaven. 'The Sea Witch is in fact . . . the Queen of the Merfolk.'

'Ha! What a twist!' snorted Horsius the Mighty. 'This sounds like some story!'

'Shhhh!' hissed Twinkle.

The Mer-mage continued. 'You must understand. Our queen loves and cares for all merfolk. But her mind was altered by darkness. While out on royal duty in the southern seas, she was ambushed by hypno-eels!'

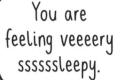

You are feeling veeeery sssssssleepy.

'They took control of her mind and ordered her to close the Singing Pearl's clam,' said the Mer-mage. 'Once she did, the eels moved into Fishopolis. And then evil beasts like giant crabs and shark guards, who for so long had been repelled by the Pearl Song, started to swim in the seas nearby.'

'And that's not all,' continued Kelp. 'The Sea Witch is capturing merfolk as prisoners and hypnotizing them into doing her bidding! I managed to escape before that happened to me. But sharks are really good at sniffing out merfolk, and that's how I ended up being chased into those crabs. '

'And why they chased us all the way to Merhaven?' asked Hoofius.

'Indeed! That's why we need your help,' said the Mer-mage. 'The Sea Witch's shark guards make easy snacks of merfolk and can sniff us out. But . . . you should be fine.'

'*Should* be?' asked Blossom.

'Well, I don't know for sure. But I doubt the sharks will have smelled anything like *you* before.'

'You can count on that,' added Trevor.

Blossom frowned at him.

'We need you to reopen the clam of the Singing Pearl,' instructed the Mer-mage. 'If you can restore the Pearl Song, it will drive away the eels and leave our Queen unharmed.'

'Hypno-eels hate loud music,' added Kelp.

'What? So we don't even get to fight this Sea Witch of yours?' said Horsius the Mighty, appalled. 'Next, you'll be telling me there's no quest reward!'

'There's no quest reward,' said the Mer-mage. 'Unless . . . you like marbles?' He pulled out a pouch and plucked a marble from it.

This one is my favourite shooter. You can't have this one!

'Opening the clam should be easy if you have the Trident of Prising,' said Kelp urgently, trying to move the conversation away from marbles.

'How could I forget?' said the Mer-mage, stowing the pouch away. 'The Trident of Prising is the most sacred legendary relic of the merfolk. We hid it deep within the Coral Caves that surround Fishopolis. Pick it up on the way in and use it to open the clam. Easy!'

PRISING BIT

SHATTERPROOF SHAFT

'A legendary relic, you say . . .' said Horsius

The Mighty, scratching his chin. He seemed interested now.

'And we'll help you find it,' said the Mer-mage. 'Conch! Bring forth the conchie-talkies!'

The merperson presented Hoofius and the old mage with a large seashell each. The Mer-mage told Hoofius to hold it up to his ear and then disappeared underwater.

Hoofius did as he was told.

CAN YOU HEAR ME, SONNY?

'Wow!' said Blossom. 'You can talk through them? I want a go!'

He snatched the shell from Hoofius and started to speak.

Hello? I'd like two sticks of candyfloss, a chocolate ice cream with extra sprinkles, and an apple juice to wash it all down.

The heroes of the Super Happy Magic Forest burst into laughter.

'Please, our second most sacred legendary relic is not a toy,' said the Mer-mage, resurfacing with a frown. 'Anyway ... IT IS TIME!'

Fishopolis awaits! May the waves watch over you and the currents carry you. And the sharks ... not eat you.

How profound.

## CHAPTER EIGHT

# INTO THE DEEP

Kelp led them through a secret underwater tunnel out of Merhaven. It was a far cry from the thrills and spills of their arrival.

'Follow the edge of the reef until you get to the Coral Caves,' she advised. 'And don't stray away from it! Danger lurks in the deep.'

She wished them good luck, and off they swam, keeping low to the reef bed and mixing in with the locals.

Hoofius was lagging behind the others and not at all happy with his mersona.

'Why did I have to get *these* things?' he complained, struggling with his jelly body and tentacles. 'They're useless and too slow!'

He flapped his way into an ocean current that started carrying him further away from the other heroes.

Ahhh! It's pulling me away!

'Oh well! It can't be helped,' said Horsius the Mighty, as the faun drifted further away. 'Only the strongest survive quests to the end.'

'We're not going on without him,' snapped Twinkle, and they all followed after.

The current carried them away from the safety of the reef's edge, and they found themselves floating among the wrecked husks of sunken pirate ships.

'I don't like the look of this,' warned Hoofius.

But Horsius the Mighty did. 'Think of all that unclaimed pirate loot, just lying around in these ruins!' He swam off to investigate the nearest shipwreck.

'You know . . .' pondered Trevor. 'We . . . could just sneak off and leave him to the loot. A natural parting of the ways.'

'No!' snapped Hoofius. 'Horsius the Mighty saved us from those bandits. Real heroes don't leave each other behind.'

The incident with the bandits had left Hoofius feeling like perhaps he wasn't good enough to lead his friends through the perils of questing. Being a pro at pan pipes and poetry wasn't the best defence against bandits with blades. But Horsius the Mighty had it all. Strength! Courage! Hooves! He was the model hero. Hoofius wanted to be just like him.

'We are lucky that such a great adventurer would want to travel with us! He can show us how to be brave and strong,' he said, as the centaur reappeared cradling a bursting chest of gold coins and jewels.

'We need to leave!' said Horsius the Mighty.

'Leave? Why?' asked Hoofius.

The heroes dashed into a nearby wreckage, squeezing through an opening too small for the serpent to follow. The serpent coiled itself around the wreckage and squeezed. The ship creaked and splintered and felt like it might cave in at any second.

'CAN'T YOU FIGHT IT?' cried Trevor to Horsius the Mighty, as beams of wood began to fall around them. But even he thought twice about taking on a foe this fierce.

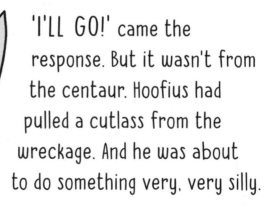

'I'LL GO!' came the response. But it wasn't from the centaur. Hoofius had pulled a cutlass from the wreckage. And he was about to do something very, very silly.

'Yes, Hoopus!' urged Horsius the Mighty . 'Defeat this foe, and you'll be Adventurer of the Year material. Just remember what I told you back on that crab island.'

'Hoofius, no!' the other heroes cried. But the faun had made up his mind. His friends needed a leader who was brave and strong and ready to battle. He'd show them all he had what it took to be a great adventurer.

Horsius the Mighty's whispered words from the island flowed through Hoofius as he swam out to face the serpent.

*And if you really want to catch them off guard . . . just throw something. Trust me. Works every time.*

Moments like this were what the greatest heroes were made of.

He swam around the ship and out of sight, hoping to surprise the beast from behind with a well-timed throw of the cutlass right between the eyes. But the closer he got, the more it seemed like a bad idea. The serpent was big enough to swallow him whole. His arm began to wobble like jelly. He tried to raise it to aim a throw, but the cutlass slipped from his grip, cutting through the water below and thudding on to the deck.

The serpent spun at the sound and began to uncoil itself from the wrecked ship.

Hoofius fled as fast as his mersona would allow him to. But he didn't get far before the serpent was upon him. It lunged with open jaws.

Hoofius dodged at the last second, and the serpent went crashing through the hull of another shipwreck.

It writhed and tried to shake itself free of the wreckage.

Hoofius didn't hang around to see if it could. He gathered the others, and together they swam as fast as they could away from the reef of wrecks.

'A fine victory!' roared Horsius the Mighty, as the wriggling sea serpent faded into the distance. 'You shall henceforth be known as . . . HOOPUS THE BRAVE!'

It wasn't exactly a masterclass in swordplay, and maybe he did get a bit lucky. But Hoofius felt himself welling up with pride regardless. He had beaten the serpent.

He was a mighty warrior after all.

CHAPTER NINE

# SUCKERS FOR PUNISHMENT

'Fishopolis,' said Herbert, tapping the enchanted compass and watching the arrow spin and then settle on their direction. They swam clear of the current and made their way back to the safety of the reef, soon finding themselves floating before the opening of the Coral Caves.

'We should be cautious,' said Herbert. 'Who knows what creatures now call these caverns home.'

'Nothing that Horsius the Mighty and Hoofius the Brave can't handle!' said Hoofius, who swam in first. He had a name to live up to, and he was rather enjoying it.

'Wow! Look at all this candy coral!' said Blossom. The caves were covered from top to bottom. He broke off a piece and began to chew enthusiastically.

BLEH!

'We're not in the Super Happy Magic Forest any more, Blossom,' said Twinkle.

The Coral Caves were a maze of caverns and tunnels designed by the ancient Fishopolisians to amplify the Pearl Song and hide their fabled city from its enemies. The merfolk could navigate them easily. Herbert rummaged in his rucksack and took out the conchie-talkie.

'Kelp? Kelp? Are you there? We're inside the Coral Caves,' said the gnome.

A few moments passed, and then the sound of their mer-friend fizzed through the shell.

'Herbert! I'm here. We're glad you made it!'

'ASK WHAT TOOK THEM SO LONG,' grumbled Barnacle the Mer-mage in the background.

Through the conchie-talkie, Kelp guided the heroes through every twist and turn as if she was there herself. But they weren't alone in the tunnels.

Can you smell something funny? It's like a unicorn crossed with a fish.

'There's a bit too much *hiding* going on for my liking,' said Hoofius, once the coast was clear. He felt emboldened by his recent triumph. 'I say we fight our way through!'

'Indeed, Hoopus the Brave!' chimed their centaur companion. 'There's no glory in sneaking. I think me you and I must be the only *true* heroes here.'

'Hey!' cried Blossom, unimpressed. 'I once fit sixty-five marshmallows in my mouth at once, thank you very much.'

'I counted as they went in,' confirmed Trevor. 'A truly heroic feat.'

The heroes rounded a corner, and their eyes popped in wonder at what stood before them.

The trident glowed in the gloom, and it wasn't until Hoofius had it in his hands that it illuminated the cave floor beneath them.

What's THIS thing?

The floor was *covered* in bones. And lots of them.

'I think we need to get out of here!' cried Twinkle.

But leaving wouldn't be so easy. Something was coming into the chamber. It made peculiar fizzing and snapping sounds.

'Get back!' ordered Hoofius to the others. 'I'll handle this!' He held up the trident, and for a moment looked every bit the warrior as they waited for whatever horror came round the corner.

And then it bobbed into view.

Ha! You're not such a scary monster, are you?

AHHHH!

The other heroes tried to wrench the creature off of their friend's face, but its arms coiled around them with suckers that shocked them with zaps of electricity.

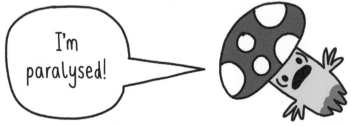

I'm paralysed!

Twinkle and Blossom had been stunned too. Only Horsius the Mighty and Herbert were still moving. The gnome was prodding and poking the beast with the wooden end of his rake, desperate to force it away.

'Help!' yelled Herbert, as the suckers curled closer along the rake handle, ready to give him a zap. 'Horsius! Help!'

Horsius the Mighty didn't usually need an invitation to fight, but right now he was holding the legendary Trident of Prising and was more interested in that than the fate of the heroes.

Herbert landed a jab to the beast's eye. It let go of Hoofius and fled through a tiny gap in the wall. The gnome grabbed a large bone and wedged it in, trapping the beast inside. Then he swam over to his friends in a panic. 'Goodness! Are any of you hurt?'

'We're okay,' said Hoofius, still struggling against the paralysis. 'No thanks to Horsius the Mighty!'

'Now, now, Hoopus!' said the centaur, eyes still fixed on the trident. 'You said you'd handle it. Besides, how are you all going to become big tough warriors if I just run in saving you all the time? A few battle scars will do you all good.'

'Heroes always help others when they need it!' replied Hoofius.

The centaur snorted. 'That's loser talk! Haven't you amateurs learnt anything from a great warrior like me? Questing is about glory and treasure! Not friendships and . . . helping! Anyway, I've got what I

came for.' He ran his fingers
along the trident.

It's not often
you get the quest
reward without
finishing the quest!

'Hey! That belongs to the merfolk!' cried
Twinkle, now floating upside down and
unable to do a thing about it.

'Not any more!' laughed Horsius the Mighty.
'It'll look fine on my mantelpiece. Do thank
them for this generous gift, if you ever
see them again.'

He turned and left, trident in hand.
Hoofius felt his heart sinking and anger
rising all at once.

'You're no hero! You're just a . . . BIG BULLY!'
He wasn't used to calling people names,
and it all came out a bit wobblier than he
had hoped.

CHAPTER TEN

# CRUNCH TIME

'Hello? Herbert? What's going on in there? Is everything okay?'

Kelp's voice echoed through the trident chamber. The conchie-talkie had been dropped amongst the bones during the chaos. And everything was very much *not okay.*

'ASK THEM IF THEY'VE DEFEATED THE SEA WITCH!' came a voice at the other end, quickly followed by a 'Shhhh!' from Kelp.

Herbert picked up the conch and filled the merfolk in on everything. 'What about my friends? Will they be okay?' he asked afterwards.

'They'll be fine,' sighed Kelp. 'Just as long as the shocktopus doesn't come back. The paralysis should wear off soon.'

Herbert was relieved to hear that at least.

'Once you're all moving again, we'll try and direct you out of there and back towards home,' said Kelp.

No.

Hoofius was straining with all his strength, his body beginning to twitch back into life.

'Unlike Horsius, we never give up on quests. We'll keep going! But . . . only if my friends still want me as their leader.' Hoofius saddened. 'I'm sorry for getting carried away with glory and battling and being strong. I feel like Hoofius the Fool.'

'Don't you mean *Hoopus* the Fool?' said Trevor with a grin. 'Just because you're our leader doesn't mean we need you to be swinging swords around and acting tough.'

'Questing is about so much more!' chimed Twinkle. 'Maybe we're not the strongest or best around, but we have always found a way, *together*.'

'Yeah! We don't need loot or swords or glory,' added Blossom.

'Just . . . each other,' finished Herbert.

Hoofius wanted to jump for joy, which was a bit of a problem when you'd lost a fight with a shocktopus.

I'd give you all a big hug if I could.

Gradually, the movement began to return to their fishy bodies, and they were able to swim their way out of the chamber without any further unfortunate incidents. Hoofius felt more determined than ever.

'Heroes, it's too dangerous,' pleaded Kelp on the conchie-talkie. 'Without the trident, you can't open the clam. For your own safety, you have to come back!'

But they had made up their minds.

'We'll find a way,' said Hoofius, as the tunnel split in front of them. 'Err . . . is it left or right here?'

Kelp directed the group through the caverns towards Fishopolis.

126

'Kelp, it's a dead end!' stammered Hoofius.

'SOMEONE MUST HAVE MOVED THE STARFISH!' shouted the Mer-mage unhelpfully.

Kelp wracked her brains, trying to figure out where she went wrong, while the heroes got themselves even more lost trying to retrace their route.

And then came voices from down the tunnel. The heroes hid amongst the coral.

Two shark guards swam by on their way back from patrol, nattering all the way.

The heroes held their breath as the sharks passed, and Herbert stuffed his hat inside the conchie-talkie to stifle any noise. The last thing they needed was the Mer-mage blathering down it and giving the sharks an easy dinner.

'They're probably going to Fishopolis,' said Blossom, after the danger had passed. 'Shouldn't we follow them? We are lost, aren't we?'

The other heroes blinked in amazement. Blossom wasn't usually an ideas unicorn unless the idea was frolicking or lunch based.

'MFFPH UMPH PHT!'

Herbert pulled his hat out of the conchie-talkie.

'HELLO? I SAID, THAT COULD WORK!'

The heroes hurried through the maze of caverns as quietly as they could, following the shark's racket. The guards grumbled mostly about being hungry, and about the Sea Witch not allowing them to eat the merfolk, which the sharks felt was all a bit unfair.

'She wants them to rebuild everything first,' said one. 'Then, we can eat them.'

'WHAT WAS THAT?' buzzed the conchie-talkie. 'HERBERT? WHO ARE YOU EATING?'

The heroes froze still. Herbert had forgotten to muffle the noise.

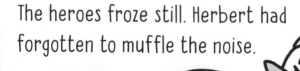

The sharks spun around, and one of them launched towards the heroes, mouth open wide.

Trevor had been right. Those swords really were unnecessary.

The first snap of the jaws missed them by inches. They weren't so lucky the second time.

It took a bite out of me!

I know how that feels.

Twinkle grabbed the conchie-talkie from Herbert and, just as the jaws opened again, she shoved it inside.

A loud crunch echoed through the caverns.

The shark shrank back as shards of shell
and sharp teeth scattered everywhere.

'Now's our chance!' called Hoofius, and the
heroes swam past the distracted guards
and through an opening in the tunnel into
brighter waters. There, they were met
with a sight that they'd never forget.

## CHAPTER ELEVEN
# SUNKEN DISORDER

The heroes hadn't been exactly sure what to expect from an ancient underwater city. They knew it'd be wet, at least. But the rest had been a mystery.

They snuck between columns of marble and old ruined buildings. There were statues too, of different fish and important merfolk from long ago. Colourful mosaics covered the floors and walls, depicting happier times when the Pearl Song serenaded the surrounding seas and kept evil at bay.

The heroes sneaked into the city, enjoying the cover and hiding spots the architecture offered as hungry shark guards prowled the waters above.

The problem was, they didn't know where to look for the Singing Pearl's clam. And they hadn't come up with a way of opening it if they found it.

*But we're here. And we're all together. That's the important thing*, Hoofius kept telling himself. He felt responsible for losing the trident to Horsius the Mighty and putting them all in greater danger, but his friends had stuck by him regardless. He had to make it up to them. *Somehow.*

Plink!  Plink!  Plink!

The sound of metal on stone snapped Hoofius back. It rang out from behind a crumbling wall.

The Sea Witch was watching over it all,
with eels atop her head.

The merfolk
are building
a new city.

Yessss!
Eelopolissss!
For eelssss!

It will
be called
Eelopolis.

'Just our luck,' groaned Hoofius. 'She's
sitting on the clam!'

'That is quite the hairstyle,' observed
Herbert, squinting.

'What do we do?' asked Twinkle. 'We can't just ask her nicely to get off while we try to open it.'

'There goes my plan,' said Blossom.

'And we can't go in there looking for fisticuffs,' added Herbert. 'We'd be shark-guard dinner in seconds . . . if the eels don't hypnotize us first, of course.'

The heroes fell silent at that thought.

Plink! Plink! Plink!

Doubts chipped away at Hoofius as he watched the merfolk working away at the statues of their new rulers.

*The statues.*

'We could create a distraction!' he said excitedly, a plan beginning to form. 'If you destroy the statues, it might draw the Sea Witch and the sharks away from the clam. Then that's my chance to open it.'

'*Your* chance?' asked Trevor.

'I have to do it,' said the faun. 'I allowed Horsius to trample all over us. You always trusted me to be your leader even though I'm not a great warrior, and I lost sight of that the moment he saved us from those bandits. Well, this time I'm not going to forget. I'm going to open that clam! What do you say?'

Was kind of hoping for a plan that didn't involve being chased by sharks. But okay.

'Meet back here for the victory pose?' asked Twinkle, hopefully.

'Of course!' smiled Hoofius. 'But first, you need to make sure to cause as much chaos and confusion as possible.'

'That should come naturally to you, Blossom,' said Herbert.

'And remember not to look at the eels if you can help it,' added Hoofius. 'That's how they hypnotize you!'

It seemed like a rather long list of ways in which things could go wrong for the heroes. But that hadn't stopped them before.

'Okay, is everyone ready?' asked Hoofius.

The heroes leapt out of hiding and did their very best to make as much of a mess as they could.

Hoofius ducked and dived his way towards the pyramid, as the bedlam at the statues began to attract the attention of every shark guard in Fishopolis.

'*Come on . . . come on . . . please . . .*' he whispered, eyes now fixed to the top of the pyramid. He had hoped that the Sea Witch would also be swimming away to investigate by now. The sharks would be upon his friends soon.

He couldn't wait forever.

Ssstop him!

Eels poked out and tried to grab Hoofius as
he flapped his way to the top. He closed his
eyes to shield himself from any attempt
at hypnotization and felt his way with his
tentacles. It turned out they were more
useful than he had first thought.

Owww!
It stingsss!

Finally, he collapsed at the top. If there
was a sea witch to battle, he might have

had to ask her to give him a minute to catch his breath.

But she was nowhere to be seen.

The Singing Pearl's clam was unguarded!

Hoofius lunged at it, putting every bit of strength he had left into prising it open.

But it wouldn't budge.

His cheeks turned purple, and his fingers went red. He almost snapped a horn. Nothing worked.

*Typical,* he thought. *The only time you need a legendary Trident of Prising, you don't have one.*

Hoofius froze still as something pointy lightly jabbed into his back, forcing him to put his hands up in surrender.

'Well, well,' came a voice. 'If it isn't Hoopus the Brave!'

## CHAPTER TWELVE
# A THREE-PRONGED ATTACK

Blossom, Herbert, Twinkle, and Trevor had run out of statues to smash, and their attention had shifted to avoiding the jaws of the Sea Witch's guards.

The plan had worked well. Almost *too* well. They were surrounded by pretty much every shark guard in Fishopolis.

'What are they waiting for?' asked Twinkle, who half expected to be lining a shark guard's belly by now.

She got the answer soon enough. The Sea Witch was arriving.

The ball of eels atop her head untangled itself, and the eels began to spin in mesmerizing circles. The heroes tried to look away, but the weapons of the shark guards left them with no choice.

It was over in moments.

From the top of the pyramid, Hoofius had the best view in town. But he had no idea what was going on around him. His eyes were fixed firmly on the sword that was being held inches from his chin.

A sword being held by Horsius the Mighty.

You're one wrong move away from a close shave.

Horsius the Mighty looked every bit worthy of his title, with his sword in one hand and the legendary Trident of Prising in the other. But there was something different about him now. Hoofius could see it in his eyes.

'Join us, Hoopus,' said the centaur. 'The Sea Witch is building a new Eelopolis and raising a great army to take over the seas. Just think of the battles . . . the glory!'

'You've been brainwashed!' responded Hoofius. 'We need to open the clam! I can help you!'

The centaur snorted. 'Help me get a promotion, more like! I'm sure the Sea Witch will be very rewarding to the champion who defended the clam from a *would-be* hero. Either way, you don't have a choice. She will be here soon, once she has finished with your friends!'

Horsius the Mighty roared with laughter. He had Hoofius right where he wanted him. But there was a sting in the tail to come.

Hoofius stretched a tentacle around and caught Horsius the Mighty on the rear.

The centaur yelped and dropped his sword, fending Hoofius and his stingy bits off with jabs of the trident.

Hoofius tried to grab it and wrench it away, and the two found themselves locked in a bitter, hairy struggle for the fate of Fishopolis.

Try as he might, Hoofius just couldn't prise the trident from Horsius the Mighty's grip, and the centaur wrestled it away again.

Hoofius was running out of time.

Horsius the Mighty lunged back at him but soon retreated when Hoofius fended him off with a sting.

'Hiding behind your tentacles, Hoopus?' cried Horsius the Mighty. 'I always knew you were a COWARD!'

But Hoofius knew what he was doing. He was goading the warrior to use his signature move.

*And if you really want to catch them off guard . . . just throw something. Trust me. Works every time.*

'Maybe it's just a draw,' taunted Hoofius. 'Maybe you're not mighty enough to beat me in battle!'

The centaur growled and unleashed a flurry of jabs at Hoofius, who dodged and put up a wall of tentacles that Horsius reared away from, frustrated. He just couldn't get close.

Hoofius readied himself. It had to be now.

Horsius the Mighty threw back his head and let out a battle cry, then launched the trident straight at him.

Hoofius dodged as the trident went soaring past him and slammed to a stop in the Singing Pearl's clam. Hoofius grabbed hold and prised it open the shell with all his might.

The seas burst into song.

LA LA LA LA LA LA LA
LA LA LA LA LA LA
LA LA LA LA LA
LA LA LA LA
LA LA LA LA
LA LA
LA

As far as songs go, it wasn't exactly Hoofius's cup of tea. Give him a jaunty pan pipe tune that you could frolic along to any day of the week. But at that moment, the song of the Singing Pearl was the best one he'd ever heard.

Though not everyone agreed. Being so close to the Pearl Song made it impossible for the eels to maintain their hypnotic hold.

And the sharks realized the eels weren't worth guarding any more.

No! Ssstop!

Mmm. I love takeaway food.

Hoofius watched it all from the pyramid top. Suddenly, he realized he had forgotten all about Horsius the Mighty. He swivelled around, in case he needed to defend himself from further attacks. But the warrior was nowhere to be seen.

Twinkle, Herbert, Blossom, and Trevor blinked at each other in a daze. The song had snapped them out of the eels' control, and they found themselves all holding pickaxes.

We must have been hypnotized and put to work crafting eel statues!

Really terrible eel statues.

Soon they were reunited with Hoofius, and he excitedly recounted the tale of his heroics to all of them as more and more merfolk gathered around to cheer and gurgle at every word.

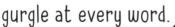

When Hoofius finished his story, a new voice could be heard above the uproar.

'On behalf of myself, the merfolk, and all the creatures who call Fishopolis home, I would like to thank you all for your heroic deeds,' said the Mer-Queen, who looked a lot

more approachable now that the wriggling ball of eels had gone from her head.

'Twinkle!' chimed Herbert. 'Didn't you say we had to meet here for something?'

'Ahh, the fish are returning!' said the Mer-
Queen. All around them the sea creatures
from Fishopolis began to filter back in
through the Coral Caves.

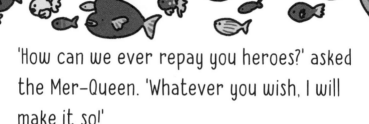

'How can we ever repay you heroes?' asked
the Mer-Queen. 'Whatever you wish, I will
make it so!'

The heroes had a quick huddle. They
weren't really used to getting quest
rewards.

'If it's okay with you, Your Majesty . . .'
began Hoofius at last. 'Could you change
us back?'

# CHAPTER THIRTEEN
# A FIN FAREWELL

A while later, the heroes found themselves back in Merhaven, wobbling around trying to stand up while getting used to having toes and hooves and foamy stems again.

Changing *out* of mersona form wasn't anything like they'd expected. There were no bubbles or gurgling or fancy ceremony. Just the Mer-mage chuckling to himself as they all fell about the place.

'We can't thank you enough, great heroes!' said Kelp. 'We'll build statues in your honour.' She was delighted to see them back unharmed and laughed off Twinkle's apology for feeding the conchie-talkie to a shark.

'Are you sure you don't want anything else?' asked the Mer-Queen, as Herbert took another tumble to the floor. 'You went to an awful lot of trouble to help us.'

'But that's what questing is all about!
We like to help those who need it if we
can,' said Hoofius, keeping his balance. He
wouldn't allow himself to forget it this
time.

'Kicking the butt of evil *is* the reward,'
said Blossom, throwing a kick and ending
up on the floor again.

The group were joined by the dolphins,
now wearing fancy armour and carrying
pointy weapons of their own. They were
all part of the Mer-Queen's newly formed
personal guard.

Permission to
squeak, your
majesty-ee-ee!

The dolphins told of capturing Horsius the Mighty as he'd tried to escape through the Coral Caves.

'Excellent work!' replied the Mer-Queen. 'I look forward to meeting this so-called hero who tried to steal our most precious relic.'

'Are you heroes ready to go home?' asked the lead dolphin. 'We'll give you a ride across the sea and up the river.'

Blossom could barely contain his excitement.

'Not again,' Herbert whimpered.

The heroes said their goodbyes to the dolphins not far from the forest border so they could get some walking practice in.

Herbert held up the enchanted compass. 'The Super Happy Magic Forest!' he declared, giving it a tap. The pointer spun and settled on the path they were walking down. 'How about that—it knows the way home!'

As they walked, figures emerged from the bushes and blocked the path in front of them. The heroes had met them before.

Hand over your stuff (again)!

But Hoofius didn't cower. Not this time.

He confidently kicked an apple tree and caught the falling fruit in his outstretched palm. He slowly drew back his arm to throw.

The bandits had seen enough.

'I suppose I did learn a few things from the five-times Adventurer of the Year,' said Hoofius, taking a bite.

They continued on to the Super Happy Magic Forest. To their surprise, everyone seemed to know they were coming.

It was a true hero's welcome. Mostly.

Woohoo!

The path through the whooping masses led them all the way to the lake where they had first found Foam, in need of help.

'Foam!' cried Twinkle, seeing her new friend's head bobbing up from the lake surface.

I missed your squishy fishy face!

'I heard the Pearl Song in faraway waters,' said a very delighted Foam. 'I figured you heroes had saved Fishopolis, and I told everyone here!'

'There's something different about you, Foam,' said Herbert, scratching his chin.

Blossom reached forward, broke off a piece of Foam's headwear, and chewed it enthusiastically.

'That's right!' gurgled Foam. 'I took a new oath. From now on I'm going to look after the candy coral here in the Super Happy Magic Forest. But you can still call me Foam. Not all merfolk are named after what they swear to protect, after all.'

'Yes, we met Dave,' said Trevor.

'ISN'T THAT JUST LOVELY!' blasted Tiddlywink on his megaphone, and everyone covered their ears. Clearly some things hadn't changed.

'I'M SURE WE CAN'T WAIT TO WELCOME FROTH INTO OUR FOREST . . .

It's Foam, you fool!

. . . BUT WHAT I WANT TO KNOW IS . . . *WHERE'S MY BOAT?*'

A sudden panic fell over the heroes, and Hoofius could feel the colour draining from his face.

'WELL?' boomed Tiddlywink. It was almost like he had been expecting this moment. What better way to ruin the heroes' party? Hoofius was struggling to get words out. He knew 'It's sitting at the bottom of the sea covered in barnacles' probably wasn't the best answer here, but it was all he had.

178

'It's . . . it's . . . ' stammered the faun.

'IT'S THERE!' cried Twinkle, amid gasps of amazement from the crowd.

Floating in the lake towards them was none other than the SS Tiddly, all patched up and with a fresh paint job to boot. It looked as good as new!

MY
BOAT!

After the tide turned in the battle for Fishopolis, Horsius the Mighty made a tactical retreat. He didn't get far.

As punishment for stealing the Legendary Trident of Prising, the Mer-Queen put him to work cleaning up after some of the muckier residents of Merhaven.

The legend of Blossom's jig lived on in the taverns of Pirate Town.

He spun on his gold horn for days. Nay—WEEKS!

While back in the Super Happy Magic Forest, Foam prepared a mer ceremony of a different kind.

I proclaim you to be... ADVENTURERS OF THE YEAR!

Woohoo!

Uh-oh.

# MATTY LONG

Hand over your stuff!

As a young boy Matty always thought he would grow up to be a game show host. But instead he became the next best thing: an illustrator and author! He has mostly made picture books and this is his first chapter book series so he hopes you like it and want to tell everyone.

When Matty is not working, he's usually telling himself he should be working. All while playing video games.

Matty lives in Ely, Cambridgeshire, and got some finsh instead.

You can find him online at www.mattylong.com.

# ALSO BY MATTY LONG